Santa Claus, Inc.

Santa Claus, Inc.

Linda Ford

SCHOLASTIC INC.

New York Toronto London Auckland Sydney

No part of this publication may be reproduced in whole or in part, or stored in a retrieval system, or transmitted in any form or by any means, electronic, mechanical, photocopying, recording, or otherwise, without written permission of the publisher. For information regarding permission, write to Scholastic Inc., 555 Broadway, New York, NY 10012.

ISBN 0-590-11504-9

12 11 10 9 8 7 6 5 4 3 2 1   7 8 9/9 0 1 2/0

Printed in the U.S.A.   40

First Scholastic printing, November 1997

To my mother, Thelma Ford
Thanks for everything

Santa Claus, Inc.

1

I will never forget the day my parents told me the truth about Santa Claus.

It was my tenth birthday, not long before Christmas. My mother sat me down at the kitchen table. My father came in to join us. He carried a briefcase and acted like this was an important business meeting. They sat on either side of the table.

"Son, there's something your mother and I need to tell you." Then Dad proceeded to lay out the facts.

Of course, I realize I was a little old to still believe in Santa Claus. I'd known all about him for years — the fake beards are dead giveaways.

Besides, in the first grade I recognized the janitor from my school earning some extra cash at the downtown mall.

"What do you want for Christmas, sonny?" he boomed in my ear, onion breath and all.

"I want the gum back that you scraped off from under my desk," I told him, grabbing my candy cane and hopping off his lap.

However, having figured out the way these things work, I thought it would be a good idea to hold on to the Santa Claus fantasy. It was all a matter of mathematics. There *had* to be extra presents in the deal. After all, when a kid believes in Santa, he gets presents in a stocking *and* under the tree *and* extras so he'll know his parents gave him something too.

A few of my friends were clued into this plan, but they weren't as good at acting as I was. They had betrayed their lack of faith by the age of eight. I was still going strong at my ninth Christmas and had figured on another bonanza year for my tenth. Until my parents put on the brakes.

My family's last name is Martin. We're your average family in an average town in the Midwest. Anywhere else and I probably couldn't have gotten away with the Santa Claus caper for so long. But people — and parents generally — think kids are more innocent in our area of the country. They aren't, but adults like to think so.

My dad worked in sales until I was in the second grade, then decided to open a flower shop. I nearly died of embarrassment; anything would have been better than flowers! Even my friends gave me a hard time. Stanley Jones, who definitely wasn't a friend, was the worst. Every day he waited by the water fountain, ready for an ambush.

"Why Rose Petal, you smell *soooooooo sweeeeeet.*" Or sometimes: "Hey, Chrysanthemum, did you ride your bike today so you could *petal* your way home?"

Who would have guessed he knew a chrysanthemum from a daisy? I figured he got it from our teacher, Mr. Canfield, whose hobby was botany. It goes to show how innocent teachers can be — giving all that ammunition to a creep without even realizing it.

My sisters didn't have it so bad. After all, girls and flowers aren't such an embarrassing combination. But even my best friend, Jake, and my other good friend, Matthew, hated to come home with me if I had to go by the shop on the way.

As it turned out, I had the last laugh. A couple of years later Dad started letting me make deliveries. The tips ran so high I gave up my paper route. There's just something about a freckle-faced kid standing at the door with a bouquet that warms the heart and opens the wallet.

During the holidays I started having more business than I could handle, and then some of my friends got the overflow. Stanley Jones, by then known as Stinko, could hardly stand it. He hung around the floral shop and hinted at his availability. I ignored him. When Dad asked me why, I told him that I had promised the job to Jake.

3

"Besides," I said, "even if Stinko made the same deliveries he wouldn't get much. *No* one could find Stinko more appealing than a dime's tip, maybe less."

"You shouldn't make fun of him. He probably can't help his breath."

"Ah, Dad, it isn't just his smell."

Dad grunted and I sighed. Like most parents, my father wants everyone to like each other and act like they live in a book. The only problem was that Stanley Jones belonged in a horror novel.

I have four, count them, *four* younger sisters. That's simply too many these days, but my parents think it's great. One of my sisters, Marcia, is my twin. It wouldn't be bad if she were the only one. She likes baseball and she isn't squeamish about taking fish off the hook. But put her together with the other girls and she's hardly bearable.

A typical day starts with the giggles.

"Do you think Mrs. Pepner will like my new dress?" says Sandy. Giggle.

"What you *really* mean is will Marcus Stephens like your new dress," teases Teresa. More giggles.

"Well, do you think he will?" Giggle.

"I think Mrs. Pepner'll like it," Teresa says. Then Sandy throws a piece of toast at Teresa.

"Maaummmm," Marcia yells. "They're throwing food again." Marcia considers herself kitchen monitor.

4

Brenda, the baby, just giggles.

"Ah, Mom," Sandy giggles when our mother comes in, "it was dry toast, not even butter on it."

"Well," Mom says, chuckling (she says she's graduated from giggling), "since there wasn't any jam involved, we'll let it go this time."

Even Marcia giggles.

I grab my lunch box and run for the door.

"Nicholas, aren't you going to walk your sisters to school?"

Mom and Dad probably should have taken me for a hearing test when I was small; they claimed I was almost deaf. Truthfully, I *could* hear Mom asking me to take Sandy and Teresa to class. But if I spent any more time with them than I already did, I'd have been crazy as well as deaf, and I wouldn't have wanted to burden my parents with so much guilt.

I have to admit that, on the whole, it wasn't as awful as it seemed at the time. At least, being the only boy, I never had to share Christmas gifts with anyone else. When Marcia started baking we always had cookies around. She wasn't a bad cook either, except for those health food recipes. And in the end, having sisters turned out to be very convenient for me.

On the whole, my life was pretty normal for a guy with four sisters and a flower shop in the family. Then Mom and Dad decided to tell me about Santa Claus.

Now, some people might think I'm making too much fuss about being told something I already knew. But those folks wouldn't understand. Mom and Dad told me the truth, the whole plain unvarnished truth.

2

"**N**icholas, darling. There's something we need to tell you — now that you're old enough to understand," said Mom, nervous and a tiny bit emotional.

"Son, you're getting too big for fairy stories about Santa." That was Dad, all business.

Uh-oh, I thought. *The jig is up.* I knew what was coming. They'd tell me I'm grown-up enough to understand the truth myself, but that I shouldn't spoil the illusions of the younger children. This would be some serious acting for me. I had to come across as surprised and disappointed, but manly enough to do my part for the little sisters.

"We know you haven't believed in Santa since you were six," Dad stated.

What? They couldn't have known! Why else would they let me get away with conning them?

"We thought it was rather fun to pretend." Mom patted my hand.

7

"Of course, it's unfortunate you recognized your janitor at the mall. Otherwise you could have had one more year before the truth caught up with you."

"Well," said Mom, "maybe, although kids do seem to wise up pretty early these days."

"I still think he might have held it for another season."

My foot tapped fast on the floor. My parents love long complicated discussions and they were quite capable of keeping me there for an hour while they debated the supposed innocence of the average American child.

"So." Dad cleared his throat. "Well, anyway, maybe we should ponder that question another time."

Mom nodded. I was relieved.

"It's time to stop pretending, son."

Terrific. They'd known I was conning them all along. Well, they couldn't ask for any of the gifts back. I'd lost or broken everything from last year except for my baseball and it looked terrible. I was so busy going over my haul from last year that I almost missed what Dad said next.

"Son, there really is a Santa Claus."

"Huh? What did you say?"

"There really is a Santa Claus."

I almost laughed, but I don't like to encourage them.

8

"Sure," I agreed. "I always knew there had to be a Santa. You only *thought* I didn't believe in him."

The joke was probably my Dad's idea. He has an awfully lame sense of humor, though Mom's isn't much better.

They looked at each other across the table for a minute while I waited for the punch line.

"Nicholas, I don't think you understand." That was Dad, completely deadpan.

"We aren't joking, dear," said Mom. "We're completely serious. Santa Claus is real."

I suddenly realized they *were* serious! Dad hadn't cracked a smile and he can never tell a joke with a straight face. Mom is almost as bad.

Dad repeated, "Santa Claus is real."

Maybe having so many sisters had warped my sanity, just as I'd always suspected. Or, even more likely, having four daughters had destroyed the brain cells of my parents. Why else would they have bought a flower shop?

"Uh-huh," I mumbled, playing along. If I could only get in touch with Grandma and Granddad. This was going to require a long stay in a padded room, or at least some regular appointments with the local psychiatrist. Having my father's parents around would help. But I was on my own. My grandparents always traveled during December and January.

"I know this comes as a surprise to you," Mom commented.

No kidding. I never thought it was possible for both of my parents to go nuts at the same time.

"But we thought it was time you knew the situation."

I felt a sudden flash of pity for my sisters. Marcia would be okay. But the brats were going to have a hard time with this.

"Do you understand?" asked Dad.

"Sure, sure," I told them and started to stand up. "If there's nothing else, I have to ... uh ..." I couldn't think. "I have uh, uh ... baseball practice!"

"In the first week of December?" Dad raised an eyebrow.

"Well, it's uh ... more like ... uh ... like preseason — "

"Sit!"

I sat.

It took two hours of talking, explaining, and showing me the proof in that briefcase before I accepted the situation. There really is a Santa Claus.

He's a business. A family business. My family: *Santa Claus, Incorporated.*

3

After the first shock I thought it was pretty cool. Santa Claus was real and someday I'd be him. Now I knew why my name was Nicholas. Before, I had thought it was just because my Dad and Granddad were named Nicholas.

The oldest son in our family is always named Nicholas. When the previous Santa gets ready to retire, his son takes his place, usually when he's about fifty years old. Our last name really should be Claus. But that would be awkward, so my great-great-grandfather legally changed it to Martin.

Grandma and Granddad aren't around much because they're too busy working for Santa Claus, Inc. The North Pole is a whole lot of miles away. During the time they do live in town, they have a normal brick house four blocks away from ours. They have a winter home up at the North Pole, sort of like a summer home at the beach, but built for cold weather. It's actually called "Santa's Castle," to fit in with tradition.

11

The busy season starts in October, getting ready for St. Nicholas's Day. This was all stuff I had to learn. Santa brings gifts on other days besides December 24th. In some countries he's expected as early as December 6th. In France he comes on New Year's Day. He helps out in countries where gifts are given on the sixth of January, even when it isn't Santa they are expecting.

Whew! There was a lot to remember, but Dad said not to worry; the family had an apprenticeship training program. In fact, Granddad had suggested I spend next summer at the Pole learning to handle the reindeer, how to avoid radar, and how to swing loop-de-loops in the sleigh. Dad said the last part with his lips twitching, so I figured it was a joke. The rest of it sounded great, though, a little like summer camp. Of course, I'd been pulling for a family trip to California next August, but that was after I'd get back anyhow.

"Sure," I said. "There aren't as many flower deliveries in the summer anyway and it's bound to be cooler up there. Wait till Jake and Matthew hear about this! Hey! Maybe they could go with me!"

"Hold on, son," Dad told me. "You can't tell anybody."

"But Matt and Jake are my best friends!"

"We understand, but not even they can know," Mom said. "If word ever got out there would be a lot of disappointed children."

"And it would wreck the family business," added Dad.

This wasn't going to be easy. Jake knew almost everything about my life. Heck, he knew stuff I'd never tell my parents!

"Promise, son?"

"Okay." I sighed. "I guess they wouldn't believe me anyway." At the moment, I wasn't sure I believed it myself. Dad patted me on the shoulder and Mom got misty-eyed again.

The Christmas season was too busy to think much about Santa Claus, Inc. Dad had the shop going like a freight train. Pine garlands with tiny white lights covered everything that didn't move. A poinsettia plant bigger than most Christmas trees stood in the corner. All the houseplants had red and green ribbons to convince customers there couldn't be a better Christmas gift than a plant — unless it's two dozen roses.

I made a mint on deliveries.

"Hello, Mrs. Jones," I'd say, flashing my best smile. "I'm Nick from Fantastic Flowers. I have a bouquet here with *your* name on it." Another big grin, a two-dollar tip, and five bouquets yet to go. On Saturdays I could handle fifteen, if my bike tire didn't go flat.

I was also pretty busy on my plan to get the family to California. I wanted to see the ocean. That was new for me. Before last fall I hadn't cared much — then I got Mrs. Williamson for fifth grade. She loved the ocean. I mean, she *really* loved it, like birds love flying and like my dad loves the idea of Santa Claus.

When I first heard the news that I'd gotten Mrs. Williamson, I wasn't exactly thrilled. She looked like she should have retired a long time ago. That first day in class, I sat back and waited for the "dear little children" speech. But, like Santa, she spoke not a word, just went straight to her work. She started with a slide show. It seemed like a good time to take a nap until she pulled some kind of electronic trick and the pictures seemed to move. A shark dived, a crab snapped, a whale spouted. Other animals did stuff too, but I didn't recognize them.

After an hour the pictures went off and the lights were turned on. Mrs. Williamson said nothing about the ocean and started on the regular stuff like reading and math.

That's how it went. The first half hour or so of class was always spent on the ocean, and she played ocean waves on her tape deck most of the time. Like I said, she *loved* the ocean. But she didn't require *us* to love the ocean. If we did, she lit up and had a great time. If we didn't, she never made us feel like there was something wrong with our likes or dislikes.

After a while I even started to enjoy the sound of the waves and wondered what it would be like to sit on a real beach. By October I was bugging Mom and Dad to consider the beach for our vacation the next summer. We generally go to the lake nearby for a week or two.

"Why not the ocean? You know, it would be a new experience," I said, using the kind of words they always employ when they want us to try new things. "It would broaden our horizons. After all, none of us have ever seen an ocean. Why, two-thirds of the planet is covered by ocean and all we've seen are pictures."

I didn't play fair; I even enlisted my sisters to help. My parents are suckers for them. I brought home extra seashells from class for the younger girls. "See?" I told Teresa and Brenda. "See the pretty shells? Wouldn't it be great to pick them up off the sand and go wading in the waves?"

Pretty soon, Teresa and Brenda started asking about the beach too.

"*Pleeeeeease*, Mom," Teresa wheedled.

"*Pleeeeeeeeeease*," added Brenda.

Mom started sending for travel brochures and studied options from the East and West Coast, also the Gulf of Mexico. Once she got real excited about Cancún — some ritzy place down south — until Dad put his foot down because it was too expensive. Mrs. Williamson suggested Monterey because there was a good sea aquarium at the wharf. The girls pressed for southern California and Disneyland. We finally settled on a week in Monterey and a week in southern California, with one day at Disneyland. What a great way to end the summer.

January is a slow month for flowers, but February is almost as good as Christmas because of Valentine's Day. Easter's good, but Mother's Day is terrific, except it only lasts one day. Before I knew it, it was time to head north. Mom packed my clothing, but I made sure of the most important things, such as my oceanography books and my new laptop computer. I'd just gotten the computer and couldn't bear to leave it behind.

Wow! Six weeks with Granddad, snow in the summer, reindeer, and elves. Time for fun!

Boy, was I ever wrong! In the first place, reindeer stink. I didn't like them and they didn't like me. At least I had an excuse; it turns out I'm allergic to them. Granddad was flabbergasted and humiliated.

"You can't be allergic! You're a Claus!"

"I . . . ah . . . ahh . . . ahhhhhchooooo . . . sure can be."

"Well, ignore it and tighten that buckle on Donner's headband."

"Maybe you could do it?"

"Why?"

"I think Donner wants to bite me."

"Don't be ridiculous. He's as harmless as a newborn kitten."

Granddad had better be right about that "kitty." He had mighty big teeth and I didn't like the way he curled his lips back over those incisors. I went forward and tackled the strap, and I learned Granddad was right . . . Donner doesn't bite. He kicks.

"What's with you?" my grandfather asked.

I spit out the mouthful of snow I'd gotten when I'd landed headfirst, five feet away from the team.

"Nothing, nothing at all!" I stated, with what little pride I could muster. After all, it was the first day and things *had* to get better.

So I thought.

4

My first week at the North Pole took most of the glamour out of the family business. I felt like I had one long cold. My feet and shins were bruised because of Donner. And there weren't any elves.

"Fairy tales, just fairy tales," Granddad explained. "Though we do employ a fair number of Laplanders."

"Short ones," I observed.

"They prefer to be called, uh ... vertically disadvantaged."

"Right. So, why aren't they making toys?"

Actually, they did everything *except* make toys. They took care of the reindeer, like reindeer cowboys, only they were called wranglers. They shoveled snow. They repaired buildings. And a huge number of them worked in the office and dealt with Santa Claus letters. But *none* of them made toys.

"We aren't in the manufacturing end," my grandfather said, "just delivery and public relations."

"Then where do the toys come from?"

"All over the world. We pick up orders and deliver on schedule."

"Who? I mean, who do we deliver for?"

"Toy makers, individuals, governments . . ."

"Governments?"

"Sure, we're big business in some countries."

"The United States?"

"Them too. The U.S. government pays us each year on November twenty-third, like clockwork. Of course, they don't make it too obvious. We're buried on some back page of the national budget, listed as a miscellaneous business inducement, line item number 1300012 . . . or something like that."

"So we do get paid."

"Of course. What do you think we are . . . stupid? You can't run a business without an income."

It took me a long time to get the whole thing straight in my head.

Governments and the big toy manufacturers pay us delivery fees. Once in a while an individual or organization pays for a special personal appearance, but that's unusual since there are so many imitators out there. The largest part of our income comes from delivery and licensing. Greeting card companies and several governments pay us licensing fees. The fees give them permission to use "Santa Claus" in government buildings, schools, and printed materials.

But our business expenses are very high. The reindeer ranch alone costs plenty and there's a lot of charity work. Security has to be pretty tight too; we have some gadgets you have to see to believe!

"Gee," I said, when my grandfather explained the antigravitational units on the sleigh, "you'd think NASA would have thought of this."

"They didn't have your great-great-great-great-grandfather on their team. He was a true genius."

"That's . . . how many years ago was that?"

"Back in 1840."

"No way. Orville and Wilbur Wright didn't even develop the airplane till *way* later than 1840."

"Forget the Wright brothers. We were the first to develop flight."

"Then why bother with handing out Christmas presents? Great-great-great-great-grandfather could have made a mint selling airplanes, or airsleighs, or whatever you want to call them."

"Never."

"Why not?" I asked. "Sounds like a good business to me. Playing Santa Claus is small potatoes compared to the aviation industry."

"In the first place, we don't 'play' Santa Claus. We are a respectable business with a long and honorable tradition. In the second place, the world needs us!"

"The world needs good air travel even more." I should have kept my mouth shut since Granddad was beginning to sound miffed, but I wasn't very happy myself.

"We simply couldn't do it. In the third place," he continued, ticking off reasons on his fingers, "the world wasn't ready for flight. In the 1840s they would have thought it was magic. They could never have understood the technology. I wouldn't risk it even now."

"Why not? I bet NASA would be able to figure it out. Maybe they could start traveling to other planets."

"I don't think the world is ready for this level of advancement."

"We can go to the moon, but we can't take reversing gravitational pulls?"

He ignored me. "In any case, like I already said, we do toy delivery and public relations, not airplane sales."

"And, besides," I said, guessing at something I suspected, "you don't really understand the technology behind it yourself, right?"

His face turned bright red and his cheeks puffed out and his eyes bulged and his nostrils nearly blew steam. Without another word he turned and stomped off in the snow.

It wasn't much of a victory. I felt bad about it. Granddad was a great guy, but he couldn't plunge a toilet, much less fix a toaster. He flew that sleigh like a professional race-car driver. He could whirl it, twirl it, go forward, backward, and sideways. He could almost loop corkscrews in that thing! But knowing how to fly it was different than understanding how it was designed and what made it work. Of course, I didn't know what made the sleigh fly either — except I hadn't been pretending I did.

To sum it up, the first week was a complete disaster.

5

Antigravity for the sleigh wasn't the only thing my ancestor invented. There was also this terrific subwave particle radio. It was all set up to be used like a telephone, but it was foolproof; no one in the world could listen in on our conversations. Not that anyone would have believed what they heard.

My parents called after I'd been there a week or so. "How are the reindeer lessons going?" Dad asked. His voice sounded just a little too casual.

"So-so." I didn't say how terrible it was. I suspected they had already gotten a report from Granddad about the whole thing.

"We'd better find you a good allergist," Mom added, confirming my suspicions.

"Can he give me a pill to make me like reindeer?"

Dad laughed like it was a good joke, but he wasn't really amused. I could understand how he felt. Santa Claus is supposed to love his reindeer.

Mom forwarded my mail. My friends were all bragging about the great things they were doing. Jake had gone to a dude ranch out West and was herding cattle for three weeks. He'd already gotten smelly, been kicked by a steer, and been chased by a heifer. It didn't seem much different from my trip — except Jake was having a good time.

The day arrived for my first flying lesson. Even though I was feuding with Donner, I was still excited. After all, no other kid I knew could fly an airplane, much less a sleigh. But before Granddad would let me fly, I had to hitch up the reindeer. All by myself.

That morning I marched out to the stable, determined to show Donner who was boss. I grabbed him by the harness. I glared straight into his black eyes. I took a deep breath and then . . . "Aaaaaa-choooo!"

Next thing I knew, I was lying on the floor of the stable. Donner had two hooves on either side of my shoulders and his nose in my face.

He belched.

I could swear he did it on purpose. No one, I repeat, *no one* has worse breath than he does. Toxic waste would smell good after being nose-to-nose with Donner.

I lost my breakfast.

Somehow I got the team harnessed. Maybe they felt sorry for me. I don't know which is worse, being pitied or being hated by reindeer. It didn't matter. By the time the team was hitched up, I was dirty, sweaty, smelly, and ready for a shower and lunch.

Of course, Granddad had no intention of waiting.

"Well, come on, boy," he bellowed. I climbed into the sleigh and we took off.

It's a good thing I'd already lost my breakfast.

This was my first time flying in the antigrav sleigh; I'd come into the North Pole by overland sled. The antigrav sleigh was nothing like a plane. Planes are solid and they don't swoop around much. But a sleigh isn't very big. It dips up and down, and swings back and forth. My stomach heaved.

"Good grief!" Granddad snorted. "Stick your head over the edge."

That was a mistake. All I could see was the ground — a *long* way down.

With a gulp, I dived onto the floor of the sleigh.

Granddad didn't realize I was afraid of heights. "Good! You're feeling better!" he insisted and hauled me back onto the seat by the collar. He shoved the reins into my hands and told me to keep the reindeer steady.

I *did* hold them steady. The reins never so much as twitched in my fingers. But Donner could tell the difference between the way Granddad held them and the way I did. He went up and then down, and then up and sideways.

I closed my eyes and hung my head over the edge again.

My sisters had been told I was away helping Grandma and Granddad on one of their trips. Once when I called, Marcia was the only one home and I broke down and told her about the Santa Claus business. Since she was family, I figured it wouldn't break security very much.

"That's terrific," she declared. As it turns out, Marcia already knew about it. She reads detective stories by the dozen and is always looking for a mystery to solve.

"How'd you know? I mean, it's not like it's your ordinary murder mystery."

"Well, you know. A clue here, a clue there."

"You mean you snuck around and listened to Mom and Dad talking."

"No . . . actually, Grandma and Granddad."

Everything about Santa Claus fascinated Marcia.

"Wow," she exclaimed, "just imagine flying that sleigh all over the world."

"I'm terrible at it."

"It was only your first try." Marcia is a born optimist. She can be really annoying sometimes. "Besides, there's more to being Santa Claus than flying a sleigh."

Marcia was right. After all, no one could be good at everything. If I couldn't fly the sleigh like the

Red Baron, I could do other things. For example, I'd been thinking about the business end of Santa Claus, Inc.

"Hey, Granddad," I said, "I've got an idea about the company."

"What is it, son?" He always called me "son" instead of "grandson."

"We don't really get enough for franchising Santa Claus. Take the United States alone. In December there are thousands of Santas everywhere. Why don't we charge them for each use?"

"Too much paperwork and government red tape," Granddad answered. "Not worth it."

"But they hardly pay us anything for how much they use our image. We could really turn this into a megabucks business."

"No." He shook his head. "It'd be too hard to track."

"Then at least we should raise our overall rates."

"We make enough money to get by."

"That's not the point," I insisted.

Granddad told me, "Don't raise your voice."

Raise my voice? Why not? He wasn't even listening to me. When I turned fifty he expected me to drop everything else to become Santa Claus, but he wouldn't pay any attention to my ideas for the company!

"We could modernize," I tried again. "We could track everything by computer."

Granddad just chuckled and turned back to his television program as though I were a two-year-old with silly ideas speaking baby words.

I gritted my teeth and went upstairs to play with my computer. It was a dandy. Two years of tips and birthday money and a loan from Dad had gone into it, but it was worth every penny.

I love computers. Computers are terrific. Computers can do all kinds of things. Computers can solve problems.

Computers can also cause problems. Big problems.

6

I never meant to cause any problems. I was just trying to help.

A couple of weeks after I arrived at the North Pole, Marcia came for a visit. I met her at the airport. She'd confronted Mom and Dad with the truth and bugged them for three days solid until they agreed to let her come.

She flew by commercial airline into Norway, then took a chartered flight to a private airfield belonging to Santa Claus, Inc. There was a two-hour wait before our air traffic controller gave us the "all clear" to take off in the sleigh. This was for security.

Delph, the air traffic controller, muttered, "Not like the good old days."

"How's it different?" Marcia asked.

"With so many commercial flights and international military jets in the air, we can hardly get around."

The sleigh can't be detected on any known radar. (Granddad nearly hit the roof when I suggested giving the technology to the U.S. Air Force as a patriotic gesture.) But it can be seen by the naked eye, so we always wait for clear airspace between the flight field and Granddad's place at the North Pole.

My stomach started knotting up as soon as I saw the airsleigh. I'd wangled a trip to the airfield in the overland sled, but it wasn't going back for another day and a half. Marcia didn't notice how pale I was getting; she was too excited. Heights never bothered her. I closed my eyes when we took off and pretended to sleep during the trip, as if I could with all the noise. Granddad and Marcia were talking a mile a minute while he showed her all the gadgets.

Fortunately, we were in the air less than half an hour. That sleigh can really move! I gulped and closed my eyes again during the landing.

The next week was pure misery. Mom had talked to an allergist, but the medicine she sent with Marcia didn't help much. I guess the doctor wasn't used to treating people for allergies to reindeer. And to top it all off, Marcia isn't allergic.

"Here you are, sweetie," she told Donner, feeding him a carrot. He acted like a kitten. And I noticed he didn't belch in *her* face.

Granddad turned and looked at me like he thought I was faking it. My nose was running. I was sneezing my head off. My eyes were swelling shut. And he thought I was *pretending* to be sick! I got *really* sick when he was turning loops in the sleigh, but I managed to get it outside.

Well, most of it.

I was determined to make things work better.

Computerizing the business seemed like a good idea, certainly more practical than a bunch of Laplanders who ran the office with the efficiency of a ground sloth. An inexpensive accounting program and a database came with my computer so I decided to make use of them.

My plan was to get Marcia to run interference while I set things up in the office. Once the system was up and running, I'd be able to give everyone the grand tour.

The head of the office was Randolph. He looked suspicious when I brought in the computer wrapped in a blanket.

"It's just a new project," I explained casually. "An idea I had for the office."

"Did you check with the boss first?"

"No, it's a surprise."

"Mr. Claus doesn't like changes."

"Don't worry. He'll like this one. Besides," I said, "I'll be the boss myself someday."

He pressed his lips tight together and stomped away. I set up the computer and got to work. The week's mail had been flown in, so I started there, entering names and addresses into the database. Norrie, who usually handled the mail, stood staring over my shoulder until I got nervous.

"It's okay, Norrie," I told him, "I don't need you right now."

"I gotta sort the mail."

"I'm doing it. See, I can record names, addresses, and gift requests on the computer in half the time you can do it by hand. After I get more practice, I can cut that down too. Next year, it'll take even *less* time since the names are already here. It'll take just a minute to update someone's file."

He humphed, looked furious, and stomped off. Later, he stood whispering to his fellow Laplanders and pointing at me. They all seemed angry. I ignored them.

"Why?" Randolph suddenly stood behind me, pointing one chubby finger onto the screen.

"Because it's more efficient," I said shortly. "See? I'm already finished. It would have taken Norrie until this afternoon."

"Norrie's a good worker."

"The computer is even better. Of course, summer mail is pretty light. Wait till you see the time it saves when the letters start pouring in."

"We always hire extra people when we need them."

"You won't need to now. And the great thing is, this is just the start. There are a lot of other things around here that we can streamline. You won't even recognize the office when we get finished."

He glared just like Norrie had and marched off to join the clutch of whispering Laplanders.

The next few days felt like pure heaven. The computer system worked like a breeze. If Granddad agreed, we could record and then start getting rid of all the old paper files cluttering up the place. As it was, letters piled up to the ceiling. Letters from the United States covered two walls, six feet deep. There were literally *millions* of letters, a lot from people who had grown up and had their own kids. Why keep a letter from a nine-year-old for forty years? But when I suggested throwing them away, Randolph acted like I was plotting murder.

"We never throw away anything Mr. Claus wants saved."

"But that was three Mr. Clauses ago! Why would Granddad even care?"

"We've always done it this way!"

Randolph looked very much like a mule at this point. Or maybe a reindeer. (I kept getting mixed up and calling him Rudolph, which didn't help our relationship.)

*   *   *

33

"And I got that baby up to three hundred miles an hour!" Marcia exclaimed.

A week had passed. Marcia spent more time with Granddad than I did and he seemed to enjoy her company. She was good at everything he showed her. On the eighth day, though, I sensed he was getting restless. After all, *I* was supposed to be learning the business and I could barely hitch up the reindeer. After seven days, not only could Marcia rein up the team, she could move 'em out. I decided to spring my surprise the next day.

Unfortunately, Granddad wasn't the only one who was surprised.

Dozens of them. I couldn't believe my eyes. There were *dozens* of short Laplanders lined up outside the window, in the snow, all carrying signs.

SAVE OUR JOBS!

UNFAIR LABOR CONDITIONS!

COMPUTERS WILL PUT ME OUT OF WORK!

The office personnel weren't the only ones out there. The reindeer wranglers raised their signs as well.

WE STRIKE AGAINST COMPUTERS!

SANTA CLAUS ISN'T A MACHINE!

REINDEER WON'T COMPUTE, NEITHER WILL WE!

GIVE THE COMPUTER AWAY, SANTA CLAUS!

"Uh . . . Granddad? Uh . . . there are some people outside."

"What? WHAT!" He stood there goggle-eyed at the scene. More people arrived by the minute, carrying signs and placards. "WE STRIKE!" was the simplistic favorite. When they saw Santa Claus at the window, they started to yell everything on their signs and a little bit more.

"Uh . . . Granddad?"

Did I say he was surprised?

It was really more like shock.

7

"**W**HAT'S GOING ON HERE?!" When Granddad came out of shock, he turned nuclear.

"They're on strike," I said as calmly as possible.

"I can see that! What I want to know is, why? And what do computers have to do with it?!"

"Oh, that. That's the terrific surprise I was telling you about. Look, Granddad, I've started to computerize the business."

I swept aside the blanket hiding the computer system and pointed to it, only a little nervous. After all, this was a *great* idea. Perhaps the computer, in all its modern glory, looked out of place among the antiques, but I had a Christmas screensaver program on it that showed Santa climbing out of the fireplace. It really looked good.

"You see?" I said, as I sat down at the computer. "Say you want to know what Susie Michaels wants for Christmas and what she asked for last year.

You just punch up her name and here it is. She wanted a teddy bear, a purse, and a doll last year. This Christmas she wants a kitten and a trip to Disneyland."

Granddad gaped at the computer screen. I punched up another file: mine.

"See, I wanted baseballs for five years running." My old letters were filed along with several million others.

A long silence inside the room. Outside, the strikers yelled and catcalled.

"Why?" Granddad asked and pointed at the computer screen, just like Rudolph, uh, I mean Randolph.

"It's more efficient. Of course, a bigger computer can do more, but this was all I could afford. Just see what this one can do and then you'll want to get something more high-powered. I'd be happy to pick it out."

Scrunching around in my chair, I examined his face. It was turning purple again.

He hissed, "Do you mean to tell me that you've been playing with this thing when you were supposed to be working with the team?"

"I wasn't playing with it. I wanted to help."

"That's what I hire people to do!"

"You won't have to hire so many now. This system is great. It'll take less than a third of our present staff."

"No wonder they're striking."

"They'll get used to it. After all, this is the twentieth century. It's about time Santa Claus, Inc. computerized. It'll save time and money."

"I already said I wasn't interested in computerizing."

"If you'd only look at it you'd see how much better it is. . . ."

This wasn't going the way I expected.

Granddad settled the strike with one fell stroke. He very publicly disconnected the computer, packed it up, and carted it to the storage shed to be shipped home.

"You're caving in to employee pressure," I protested. "After all, *you* are the employer. You have a right to run your business the way *you* want to run it."

"I *am* running it the way I want to," he stated. "I don't want a computer any more than they do."

With the disappearance of the computer, the situation returned to normal. In other words, Donner and I continued our feud and I kept getting airsick. Granddad gave me assignments every night to memorize maps, air schedules, and the local Santa Claus customs in each country. The next day he'd grill me on my lessons.

"When is St. Nicholas's Day in the Netherlands?"

"December sixth."

"Who gives gifts in Syria?"

"The Wise Men's youngest camel."

"What's the highest mountain peak between the North Pole and Los Angeles?"

"Uh . . ."

"I thought you studied this!"

"I did!"

Whenever I needed something from the office Randolph and Norrie gave me the super-cold-freeze silent treatment. Not that they ever refused whatever I needed, they just acted like I was beneath them. They were the winners and I was the loser.

The thing that got to me was that no one gave me credit for trying to fit into the business. No one figured Donner might have something to do with the problems we were having. No one cared that I lost my lunch every time I went up in the sleigh. Granddad just told me to stick my head in a sack since he didn't want another clean-up job.

Two days later, Mom and Dad flew in for an unscheduled visit. Granddad had called in the cavalry. Dad started giving me up-and-at-'em pep talks. Mom gave me understanding smiles and consoling pats on the shoulder. They both drove me crazy.

"Why don't you send me to a psychiatrist?" I asked one evening.

"What for?" Mom looked confused.

"To learn to like reindeer, of course. Can't you

just picture the doctor's face when you tell him you want me psychoanalyzed because I don't like Santa's reindeer team?"

They chuckled politely. It wasn't a good joke. In fact, it wasn't a joke at all. I hoped I wasn't turning out as deadly dull as my parents.

Dad lost some of his patience and pep when Granddad told him about the strike. Maybe I should have mentioned it first, because he wasn't interested in my side afterward.

"I suppose you meant well, Nick," said Dad. "But that just isn't the way we run the business."

"What do you mean *we*?!" I growled. "No one's interested in what *I* have to say about it."

"You're still learning. We'll teach you to do it the right way."

The right way? They meant *their* way.

8

When I saw Mom and Dad off at the airport, Dad said, "Make us proud, son," clasping me on the shoulder. Everything he expected from me was in the weight of that arm across my shoulder blades. He had boasted that on the first summer of his apprenticeship he flew the sleigh at two hundred miles per hour, looped simple to moderately difficult maneuvers, and had the international Santa Claus schedule memorized. He obviously expected more from me than he was getting.

On the way back to the North Pole I loaded up on good intentions. Not that they helped me much. No matter how hard I worked, I wasn't any *good* at it. The geography and book work weren't too bad, since I'm an okay student, but with any of the practical "hands-on" stuff I kept flubbing my way through. I finally learned to fly the sleigh — slowly. I couldn't manage any fancy maneuvers. At most, the reindeer team and I formed an uneasy truce.

"Come on, Nick!" Granddad kept yelling at me. "The team has to know who's in charge."

I already knew.

They were.

Apart from the tension of going up in the air without any ground to stand on, I started to find the whole thing rather boring. That's a horrible thing to admit, I guess. Granddad thinks it's the most exciting job in the world. But to me, being Santa was just the same thing over and over and over again, nothing else. Maybe it was because I had to do it all their way, with no opinions of my own. Can you believe it? It made me wish Granddad was more like Mrs. Williamson. In class, if I had an idea about how to do something, she let me try it. Sometimes it worked, sometimes it didn't. But it was fun finding out for myself. Added to that, the ocean really *is* interesting.

"Hey, Granddad, did you know that if you chop a starfish into pieces, the pieces will grow back into separate whole starfishes?"

"Starfish," he said. "It's starfish, not starfishes. Why can't they teach grammar in today's schools?"

"Actually, Granddad, it can be both. Either starfish or starfishes is correct." I knew I was right because I'd done a report on starfish for Mrs. Williamson.

"Nonsense," Granddad growled. "It's starfish."

I insisted, "Really, check it out."

42

"Ridiculous."

Naturally, he refused to pull out the dictionary. He just expected me to consider him right, and me wrong — no matter what. Maybe it was because he was older, or maybe it was because he was Santa Claus and he figured he had status. Considering that the whole world thought Santa Claus was perfect, he may have concluded it was his right to always be right, even when he wasn't.

Actually, I'd been doing a lot of thinking about the way the world looks at Santa. Not everyone thinks he's perfect. Look at the "Rudolph the Red-Nosed Reindeer" story, where Santa turned out to be prejudiced against shiny red noses. I was starting to like stories that made Santa Claus less than a hero, which just goes to show how far down I'd gone.

I was careful to keep my thoughts to myself. The North Pole staff would probably picket *me* if they knew what I was thinking. It wasn't too hard to keep my mouth shut, even though I had to work in the office for several days. I was still in the doghouse with the Laplanders. But it was better than flying lessons in the sleigh, and something interesting did happen while I was there. Two things in fact. The first was the letter from the CIA.

"What's this?" A letter had fallen out from one of the bundles from the United States.

I was moving boxes, like your ordinary moving man. Granddad must have figured I couldn't do any harm that way. The letter I found wasn't your ordinary gift request list. The return address read *United States Government.* Since the computer fiasco, I hadn't paid much attention to the business side of things. However, this looked interesting. TOP SECRET was stamped in red letters on the envelope.

Granddad probably wouldn't want me to read it, but I didn't care. I snuck into a corner and opened the envelope. My jaw nearly dropped to the floor. Ten years ago, the CIA actually wrote to my grandfather! The real CIA! The Central Intelligence Agency of the United States! The people who spy for the government!

They had asked him to keep an eye on certain nations for them. Think of that! My grandfather, the *secret agent*, like James Bond, only older and fatter. The great thing was, this made sense. Granddad had a sleigh that couldn't be detected by radar. No one would suspect a guy in a white beard and a red suit anyway. I hunted my grandfather down and got him off by himself.

"Wow! Granddad. This is really neat!" I waved the letter at him.

"Huh, what?"

"This!" I settled down and handed him the letter.

"Oh," was all he said.

"What do you mean, 'oh.' This is big! This is awesome. This is incredible!"

"Where'd you get it?"

"In with the other 'Dear Santa' letters. I guess you're glad to get it back. Shouldn't we burn it, or eat it, or something?" I asked.

"Just throw it back in with the stuff on my desk."

I couldn't believe he was so easygoing about this.

"But . . . what if someone finds it and learns you're a spy?"

"What? Good grief, Nick, you don't really think I'd do something like that!"

"Oh, I get it," I said, nodding wisely and lowering my voice to a whisper. "No one's supposed to know."

"Good glory and antelope whiskers," he exploded. "You can't imagine I'd use the honor and love of Santa Claus in order to spy on people!"

"What about the letter?"

"They asked, but I turned them down flat."

I should have realized it earlier. My grandfather is far too stuffy to ever become James Bond. To be honest, I suppose I could see his point. Santa Claus and trench coats don't really go together. At the same time, I was disappointed. For a short time being Santa Claus had looked exciting, dangerous, and glamorous.

The second interesting thing that happened turned an average rotten day into another big disaster.

9

Marcia had spent the day before with Grand-dad and she had emerged from the sleigh beaming with pride. He said she had a natural knack for flying, unlike certain other members of the Claus family. I ignored that remark. I already knew Marcia was a better pilot. She was *born* to be a better pilot. I'd rather keep my feet on the ground, or maybe take a dive in the ocean. Flying was for the birds. Needless to say, my opinion held no weight with Granddad.

"I'll teach you if it takes the next forty years," he stated. "I'll teach you if it takes the rest of my life."

Great, just great. I could see myself at age fifty, still a rookie apprentice in the family business, still getting yelled at, pushed around, humiliated, and airsick.

I retreated to my room and spent the evening reading about whales. Granddad thought I was studying the Spanish customs of Christmas gift-giving. I kept the book handy, ready to pretend I was reading it if he came to the door. Surely I could take one evening off for something I liked.

I couldn't blame Marcia for the trouble. She couldn't help the fact she was good at everything I wasn't. It wasn't her fault that Granddad kept comparing us, hinting that I was just lazy and didn't try hard enough.

It's not that my grandfather is a bad person. Despite our troubles I really love him. He's a fair employer. He loves children and old people. He loves his family. He's nice to animals.

But he has this one little blind spot: ME! He can't accept that I'm not very good at being Santa and that I might *never* be good at it.

Granddad has one other fault as well. But no one had ever noticed it until I opened my big mouth.

The next day I moped around the office. Granddad had tested me on my knowledge of Spanish Christmas customs after all. If he had examined me on the migration patterns of the gray whale I'd have done fine. But I didn't have a clue about Spain.

"Who gives gifts in Spain?"

"Uhhhh . . . Le Père Noel?" I guessed.

"That's France!"

47

Well, Spain and France were connected. How could two countries so close together be so different?

"Hmmmmm, hummmm, de hummmmm." Marcia pretended she wasn't paying attention and was just humming for fun, but I knew better. The tune was "Three Blind Mice." She was trying to give me a hint. It couldn't be the blind mice, so it had to be the number three. Three . . .

"Three . . . uhhhhh . . . the Three Kings?" I vaguely remembered that some people in certain countries believed the Three Kings from the Bible story gave them their Christmas gifts.

"Humphfff!" Granddad stalked off, but my sister gave me the thumbs-up sign so I guess I'd given the correct answer.

"Thanks," I said.

She grinned and ran outside to the waiting sleigh. Granddad had promised she could fly it solo that morning.

With Marcia in the air and my grandfather off sulking, I didn't have much to do, so I wandered outside. Once upon a time I had thought it would be great staying at the North Pole. The Midwest of the United States can be awfully hot and sticky in the summer. Snow and the North Pole seemed like heaven compared to that. But after five weeks of working in the snow, I really missed heat and swimming pools and grass growing. I missed getting so hot and sweaty you can hardly bear it, then standing in line for a frozen juice bar.

"Hello?" A glum voice interrupted my sweaty memories.

I turned around and looked . . . up. The stranger standing beside me was tall, at least six feet. After weeks of working around short people, he seemed rather like a giant. He looked as depressed as I felt.

"Something wrong?" I asked.

He nodded and sighed. "I was hoping . . . well, I was hoping to get a job. But I'm too tall."

"What d'you mean?"

"I couldn't walk under the 'elf' sign."

Elf sign. Yeah, there was a signpost with a white sign sticking out that said: ELVES. I thought it was kind of silly, considering there were no elves at Santa's Castle, but had figured it was one of my dad's lame jokes.

"You mean you can't work here unless you can walk under that short little sign?"

He nodded again.

"Why, why," I sputtered. "That's not right. They can't refuse to hire you just because you're tall."

"Really?" The man brightened up and looked hopeful. "Just wait till I tell Olaf and Jon and Peter about this . . . and Vladmir and . . ." He turned and strode away.

Oh, no. I'd done it again.

* * *

There were hoards of them. They carried big signs and posters:

UNFAIR HIRING PRACTICES!

DISCRIMINATION!

SANTA ISN'T AN EQUAL OPPORTUNITY EMPLOYER!

There were also signs in another language. All the people who worked for Santa Claus, Inc. are required to learn English, but some of these obviously couldn't speak it yet.

"What?!" For the second time that summer, Granddad went into shock.

I must have looked guilty, because when he came out of it, he turned to me. "Nick. What do you know about this?"

"Well, uhhhhhhh, I just happened to mention uhhh . . ."

"You just happened to mention what?" he repeated sarcastically.

"That, uh, uh, that being tall shouldn't be . . . uh, a factor in hiring someone."

"I've always hired short people! It keeps the atmosphere more traditional."

"You mean elves?"

"Yes!"

"But you don't have any elves and you never have had any elves. Don't you think they have a right to call it unfair?" I pointed to the group outside. When I'd first seen them, I admit I considered telling my grandfather I knew nothing about the situation. But this was about justice. Grand-dad *was* being unfair.

I marched outside and joined the hoard, picking up an extra sign. "Unfair," I shouted, partly for them and partly for myself.

10

Santa's Castle would never be the same.

After a short negotiation, Granddad gave in and agreed to hire tall people along with short ones. When I suggested he take the "elves" sign down and destroy it as a symbolic gesture, he glared and then ripped it into shreds. Then he stalked off toward the reindeer barns. I hid in my room the rest of the day. Grandma sneaked me up some supper, a serious breach of her own rules; usually she allowed no eating outside of the kitchen or dining room.

"Don't worry, Nicky." She sat down on the bed beside me. "Things will work out. You'll see. Besides," she said, "it was a good thing that happened today."

That shocked me. Never had Grandma shown anything but one hundred percent agreement with Granddad. I always thought she was like a rubber stamp of approval on whatever he said and did.

She hugged me tight and quietly departed. I wolfed down my food. With everything that had happened I thought I'd lost my appetite. But something about the way Grandma smiled brought it back.

Marcia peeked around the door a few minutes later. "Ooooooh," she said. "If Grandma finds out, you'll really be in hot water. You don't know what trouble is till Grandma gets mad."

"Smarty." I smirked. "Grandma brought it."

"Congratulations!" She applauded. "She either feels sorry for you or she's on your side."

"Not if Granddad has anything to say about it."

She perched on my bed and plucked a cookie off my dessert plate. I didn't mind sharing. Grandma had brought a pile of them.

"How'd the solo go?" I asked.

"Great!" Marcia beamed. "I got a whole two hours in the air and did a lot of fancy stuff. I even," she lowered her voice, "I even did a mobus. And I did it right!"

"Marcia! You could have been killed! Even Granddad can't do one of those."

"Well, I did one!"

She looked and sounded smug and she had a right to be. A mobus is really hard. It's like a figure eight and a corkscrew combined. Granddad had been working on the same maneuver for the last *forty-five years*. I'll never manage one if I live to be a hundred and fifty.

"I'm impressed."

She shrugged and tried, unsuccessfully, to look modest.

"I hear you had an exciting day too," she commented.

I groaned and hid my head under the pillow.

The next day, Granddad hauled me out of bed before the crack of dawn and had me down at the stable.

"Harness them up," he grunted and stomped off. I swallowed carefully. Just the thought of going up in the sleigh made me taste last night's dinner again.

"Hi." Marcia's voice startled me. She looked bright and wide awake, while I felt like a beached whale. Whenever I got near the reindeer my eyes itched and my nose felt like it was going to explode. I don't know why they were so surprised about my allergies. Everyone in my family is allergic to *something*. It was only a matter of time until reindeer got on the list.

I kept my eye on Donner. Marcia was petting him and he was rubbing his head on her shoulder like a cat rubs against your ankles. He glanced my way and looked positively smug.

Okay. Maybe I was getting paranoid. But I'd swear Donner was out to get me.

*   *   *

Donner got me. Grandpa insisted I go solo. He had to be nuts, but he kept saying that the reindeer knew what to do, even if I didn't.

They sure did know what to do . . . and they didn't pay any attention to anything *I* did. Then, when we touched down on the snow, I pulled on the reins to slow the team. Donner snorted and all the reindeer stopped short.

The sleigh doesn't have seat belts.

It stopped.

I didn't.

Randolph laughed himself sick when he saw my black eye.

Of course, I couldn't swear that Donner did it deliberately. I'm pretty clumsy with the reins and *could* have pulled too hard. But it still seems mighty suspicious that it was the first time the team did anything I asked them to do during that whole solo flight.

Granddad just said it was the price of learning new skills and not to worry, he'd whip me into shape if it was the last thing he'd do. I *already* felt whipped.

11

I was ecstatic when the six weeks were up and I could go home. Marcia wasn't as thrilled as me, although Granddad let her fly the sleigh to the airport. Thankfully, she resisted any loop-de-loops since I was in the back.

For the first time, my stomach didn't have problems. I was too happy to be leaving — and too excited about finally getting to go to California. Mom and Dad met us at the San Francisco Airport and we headed for Monterey.

The ocean was fabulous! It rolled and it rolled and it never got tired. I also saw all sorts of cool stuff at the aquarium.

"Look," I shouted. They had an actual shark in a tank.

"Uggghhh," Mom said. The girls squealed.

"Ugly thing, isn't it?" Dad commented and walked away.

How could they? How could they walk past it like it was some commonplace pot of flowers?

Sure, he was ugly; that's part of what made him so beautiful. He was a leftover, a holdover from more primitive days, like a living fossil.

Behind the glass, the mean greedy eyes searched constantly for something to eat. Sharks are always hungry; something about their stomachs won't let them rest. In the aquarium this one didn't have to hunt. They fed him plenty of food every day. I wondered if he would rather have his freedom than a steady food supply. He was trapped in a cushy job he probably didn't want. I knew how he felt. I felt the same way.

If it was up to me we would have spent days and days at the aquarium. The rest of the family didn't agree

Swimming in the ocean was great too. In fact, everything about the ocean is terrific. I could hardly stand it when the two weeks were up and we flew home.

"You know what?" I asked casually one evening, a few days after getting back from California. I'd been practicing being casual in front of my mirror.

"No, what's his last name?" Dad smirked, thinking himself funny. Why did the girls have to encourage him by giggling?

"Well," I said, ignoring them, "I think maybe I'd like to major in oceanography when I go to college."

"Hmmm." Dad yawned. It was getting close to his bedtime. "Hardly worth it, don't you think?

Hobbies are nice, but you'd better study something useful. Besides, you have lots of time."

"But this *is* useful, Dad," I stated, trying to keep that casual tone. "I could become an oceanographer, maybe do research, or even teach."

"Yes, but it wouldn't be useful for *you*." Dad yawned again. "You'd put all that preparation into something you could only do part-time for a few years. It's better to pick a more practical area of study."

There it was, the whole problem in a nutshell. I couldn't do what I really wanted because someday I was supposed to be Santa Claus. The honest truth was that I didn't *want* to be Santa Claus, but I was stuck with the job.

12

I've seen television shows about pushy parents — the kind that prod their kids into stuff like sports or acting. You see them at Little League games. Their kid has to be the best, no matter what.

I've always been grateful for my dad, who not only says baseball is a game to enjoy but means it. If I want help practicing, he is glad to pitch or catch for me. If I don't want to practice, no problem. He cheers for my team and has fun catcalling the umpire. But it is just for fun.

Unfortunately, Santa Claus, Inc. isn't a game to my father, or to Granddad. It is a serious business enterprise which provides a full income for my grandparents and a partial income for us. College tuition would come from Santa, and other funds would give the girls a "start in life," as Dad put it. We didn't actually need the money; the flower shop was quite successful. This surprised Dad. I think he thought of selling flowers as more of a hobby until his *real* career started.

"A man has to have a job," he always said. "He needs to get up in the morning and have some kind of work to do. When Granddad retires and I take over as Santa," he told me, "you'll be ready to manage the shop."

How can parents be so blind? The last thing I wanted to do was run a flower shop that didn't even belong to me. Dad wanted to be his own boss and mine too. The family had my entire life mapped out and expected me to be thrilled about it.

For six generations the oldest son in our family gladly became Santa Claus. It was like a royal privilege. It was like the throne of England, my parents said, only better because there were other thrones and many kings in the world, but there was only one Santa Claus.

It was also a royal pain.

Mom had a family barbecue after my grandparents got back from the North Pole.

"How do you like 'em?" Dad wielded the spatula. He wore a big chef's hat and one of those silly aprons with a stupid saying on it. "Charred, burned, or cremated?" he asked and held up a coal-black hot dog nobody wanted. It had been forgotten while the chicken cooked. Chicken, potato salad, beans, and one watermelon later, the adults, Marcia, and I sat around the patio looking sleepy. Everyone was relaxed except me. I had eaten almost nothing, waiting for a good time to make my move. I couldn't find a good time so I just blurted it out:

"Say, what would happen," I began, "if I didn't become Santa Claus?"

Five suddenly unrelaxed heads swung around and ten eyes examined me like a bug under a microscope.

"That isn't funny," my father snapped.

"Don't even joke about such a thing," said Granddad.

Mom seemed to be in shock. Grandma raised her eyebrows and Marcia stared at me with no expression on her face.

"Actually," I said, scraping up my courage, "I wasn't joking and I don't think it's funny either." I think Granddad was about to have apoplexy . . . whatever that is.

"Nicky, darling," Mom protested, coming out of her daze, "you can't mean such a thing."

Dad said, "The family's counting on you."

"Good grief!" Granddad roared. "The whole world is counting on you. You're the only Nicholas Claus left!"

"I want to be an oceanographer, not Santa Claus!"

"Anyone can do that. Only you can be Santa!"

"It's such a privilege," Mom stated, getting emotional.

"It's your heritage," Dad said.

Granddad yelled, "It's your job!"

I felt terrible and selfish and mean. I felt like dirty gum stuck on a shoe. I felt like a scum-sucking pig.

"I think," Grandma said in her gentle voice, "that it's a good idea for everyone to quiet down and let Nicky tell us how he feels. Let's talk with him instead of everybody yelling their heads off."

Grandma never said things like "shut up," but that's what she meant and that's what everyone did. After a few minutes of contemplating my dirty bare feet, I said it again.

"I want to be an oceanographer."

No response.

"I'm allergic to reindeer. They don't like me and I don't like them. I can't fly well. I don't like the cold. I get airsick and what's more, I . . ."

The last was difficult to admit, but I had to make a clean confession to get them to listen to me.

". . . I'm scared of going up so high."

My grandfather seemed offended but kept quiet after a look from Grandma.

"The worst part of it is, I find the whole thing boring."

"Santa Claus boring?" Mom asked sadly.

"I think," Dad said in a kind of voice you use with tiny children, "that you're confused. I know how hard you've tried and that you've had a rough time learning everything. But when things get difficult you just need to try harder. Don't be a quitter. You know what they say about quitters, don't you?"

Mom offered hesitantly, "Well, maybe . . . perhaps he could ease up on his Santa Claus studies. Maybe we've pushed him too hard."

"That's the ticket!" Dad agreed. "He needs a vacation. Then next year he can really buckle down and make everything work. What do you say?" he asked Granddad.

"As long as we don't hear any more of this ridiculous nonsense."

"Oh, I'm sure this thing about the ocean is just because he feels too much pressure. He won't let us down. He won't let the whole world down, will you, Nick?"

I was trapped.

13

"It won't make any difference."

"What won't?" Marcia asked.

We were alone in my room. Granddad and Grandma had gone home. The rest of the family was in bed, probably fast asleep. I'm the only night person in the family. Even Marcia was yawning and it was only nine-thirty at night.

"Taking a summer off won't help," I explained. "And it isn't just because I'm allergic to reindeer. I don't want to be Santa."

Marcia just picked at the lint on my bedspread. She acted as if she didn't want to discuss the subject. Maybe she thought I was a selfish pig too. It made me feel even worse.

My folks called it a vacation from Santa Claus training. I called it horrible. I'm sure they didn't mean to make me miserable. They simply couldn't understand how I felt. They had offered me the most wonderful thing they could think of and I didn't want it.

Marcia had started to avoid me, spending a lot of time with her friends or in her room or at the library. One of Sandy's friends had started to be a pain, hanging around and making goo-goo eyes at me. I was tempted to tell her that if we ever got married she'd have to put on fifty pounds, cook for the Laplanders, and wear fuddy-duddy old dresses half the year while she played Mrs. Santa Claus.

I kept my oceanography books out of sight. I even pulled out Santa Claus schedules and studied them in front of everyone so they'd know I was trying. There may have been a martyred look on my face, but I did make an effort.

My parents weren't satisfied. They didn't want me just to agree to take over the family business; they wanted me to be happy about it. After all, Santa Claus is supposed to be jolly.

"You'll see," my dad said in one of his regular pep talks. "Everything will turn out fine. I didn't want to admit it before, but I had trouble in the beginning too."

"Oh really?" I asked.

"Sure, sure. I brag like it was a breeze, but flying that sleigh is tough."

I'm pretty sure he wasn't telling the truth. It showed how much he cared about the business to make himself look bad.

"You were born to be Santa Claus, Nick," he said heartily. "You only thought oceanography was what you wanted because you hit some snags in your training."

I couldn't bring myself to tell him that even if I didn't want to be an oceanographer, I still wouldn't want to be Santa.

"You can do so much good in the world as Santa Claus," Mom would say, trying another angle. "People need to believe in giving and sharing and generosity, and they need to see someone who shows the spirit of love at Christmastime. Not that Santa is the only one who does that." Mom always had to be honest. "But he's very good at it."

I couldn't resist saying, "The world needs oceanographers too."

"I'm sure they do —"

"Just think of how important it is," I interrupted. "The ocean plants make a lot of the oxygen we breathe. Plenty of food comes from the sea. Maybe oceanography can help cure world hunger. And there's pollution in the ocean. We need people to study it and try to help."

"I know, Nick," she said, "but anyone could do that kind of work. Only you can be Santa Claus."

Only you, only you, only you, only you. The words hammered into my brain. I dreamed them at night and heard them all day. If my parents didn't say them, they thought them.

Why couldn't I have an older brother? Or an

uncle whose son would just love to take over? Why did it have to be only me? Only me . . .

I knew I had to think of something.

"Hi, Marcia." She had come in the back door and found me having chocolate chip cookies and milk at the breakfast table.

I pushed the plate of cookies toward her. She hesitated, then poured herself a glass of milk and sat down.

"You mad at me or something?" I asked.

"Huh?" She looked honestly surprised.

"You've been ignoring me. I never see you."

"I've been busy. Anyhow, I thought you liked it when your sisters were invisible." She grinned.

"You're not so awful."

"Thanks for the compliment."

"I thought maybe you were mad because of what I said about being Santa Claus. Mom and Dad are still upset."

"Well, I'm not."

"I just don't know what to do, Marcia," I said. "I don't want to let the family down, but I also don't want to be Santa Claus. I'm lousy at it. You've seen me! You're the one who's really good at it."

She looked uncomfortable. There was a cookie in her hand and she started crumbling it into pieces, picking out the chocolate chips and the nuts, piling chips, nuts, and crumbs in separate heaps on her plate. Maybe she was embarrassed. She was a nice person, so maybe she felt bad because she made me look worse at the Santa Claus stuff. Or maybe . . .

"Hey, Marcia," I asked softly, "would you like to be Santa Claus?"

14

Once I asked the question, I could see it was what Marcia really wanted. I should have seen it a long time ago.

"What?" She tried to be casual.

"Wouldn't you like to become Santa Claus?"

"I'm not a guy."

True. Everyone thought of Santa as a man, but who could see under that suit and beard anyway? "So what?" I shrugged.

She looked up from the mess she was making. "Do you really think I could?"

"You're already a hundred times better at it than me."

"Oh, Nick," she finally confessed, "I'd love it. But I don't want to steal it away from you."

"Steal it? You're welcome to it. I don't want it at any price."

"Mom and Dad are sure you'll change your mind."

"They need their heads examined."

After another hour, Marcia was finally convinced. The family took much longer.

"Ridiculous," Granddad roared.

"Don't be silly," my father added.

"I know you're just trying to help your brother," said my mom to my sister.

"I really want the job," Marcia declared.

I insisted, "I really *don't* want the job."

"It's man's work!" Granddad proclaimed.

"This is the twentieth century," I answered. "You can't say things like that."

"I think you're both being silly," said Mom.

"The whole concept is absurd," Dad announced.

Grandma stated loudly, "I think it's a good idea!"

Sudden silence. Everyone turned to stare at the little silver-haired lady who usually just watched our family arguments.

"You're not serious?" Granddad asked.

"She's good at it. As hard as Nicky tries . . . and he does try very hard . . ." She looked pointedly at Granddad. "As hard as he tries, he doesn't have Marcia's talent for the job."

"But . . ." Dad didn't seem to know what to say.

"We'll be a laughingstock," Granddad muttered.

"I don't know about that," Grandma disagreed. "All over the world women are trying new things."

Granddad reminded her, "She can't grow a beard."

"Neither can you."

I snickered. Grandma had him there. His own beard was so scraggly, he'd finally given up and gotten a specially manufactured one.

"Nicky, go be an oceanographer." Grandma nodded at me. "Or, if you change your mind and decide on something else, go be the best you can and make the world better in your own way. I'm proud of you, son. It took guts to admit you didn't want to be Santa. Marcia, you'll be the best Santa we've ever had."

Victory was on Grandma's face. She had settled the decision for the entire family.

Actually, it took a little longer than one evening's argument to get Dad and Granddad to come around. They backtracked the next day, but Grandma is like an unmovable force. Once she decides something, she's stronger than anyone I've ever known. I guess Granddad and my father knew they were licked from the beginning, but they had to resist a while to save face.

So, that's how a girl turned out to be Santa Claus. Or at least she will be in thirty or forty years.

"You're the greatest, Nick," Marcia stated when we were alone again.

I shrugged modestly. "It's nothing."

"By the way, when the time comes will you help us computerize?"

I gaped at her, dumbfounded. She grinned.

"Of course, I'm not stupid enough to try and force one on Granddad right now," she said. "But just wait till I'm in charge."

I bet by the time she's in charge she won't even have to wear the beard.

Now, for anyone who prefers it the old way where Santa Claus was always a man? All I can say is that they never saw Marcia fly that sleigh.